D1442300

FAVORITE MOTHER GOOSE RHYMES

Little Bo Peep

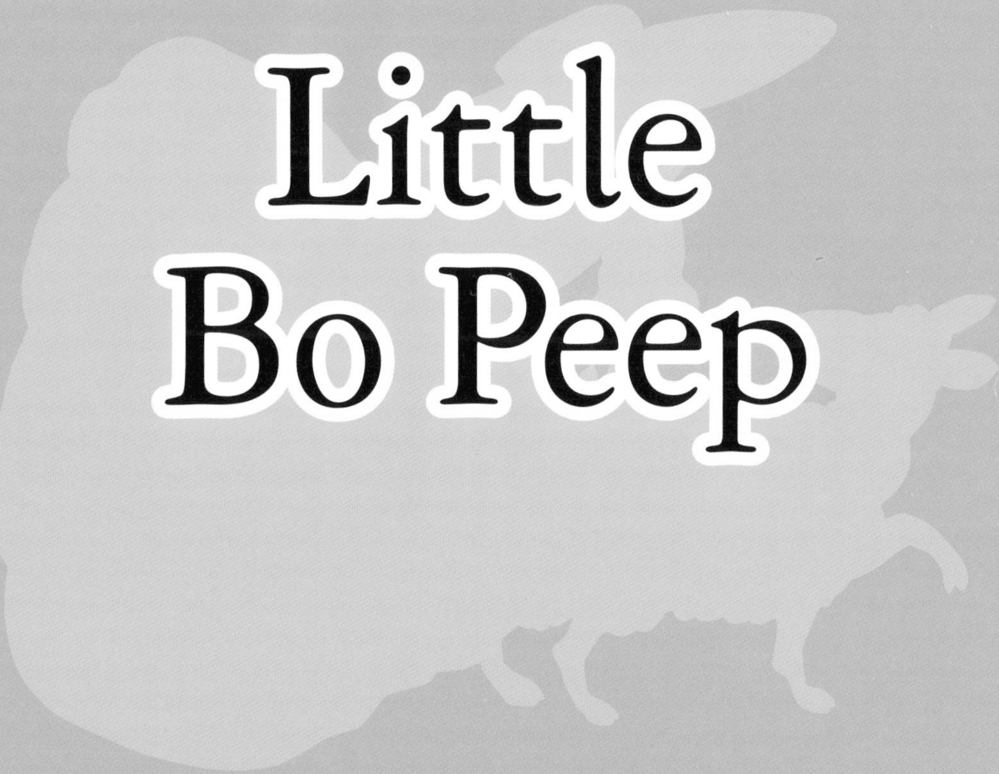

The Child's World®

Published in the United States of America by The Child's World®
1980 Lookout Drive • Mankato, MN 56003-1705
800-599-READ • www.childsworld.com

Acknowledgments
The Child's World®: Mary Berendes, Publishing Director
Editorial Directions: E. Russell Primm, Editor; Lucia Raatma, Proofreader
The Design Lab: Kathleen Petelinsek, Art Direction and Design;
  Anna Petelinsek and Victoria Stanley, Page Production

Library of Congress Cataloging-in-Publication Data
Woodruff, Liza.
  Little Bo Peep / illustrated by Liza Woodruff.
      p. cm. — (Favorite Mother Goose rhymes)
  Summary: Presents the classic nursery rhyme about the little girl who lost
her sheep.
  ISBN 978-1-60253-302-8 (library bound : alk. paper)
  1. Nursery rhymes. 2. Children's poetry. [1. Nursery rhymes.]
I. Mother Goose. II. Title. III. Series.
  PZ8.3.W8919Li 2009
  398.8—dc22   2009001562

ILLUSTRATED BY LIZA WOODRUFF

Little Bo Peep has lost her sheep,
and can't tell where to find them.

Leave them alone,
and they'll come home,
wagging their tails
behind them.

5

Little Bo Peep fell fast asleep, and dreamt she heard them bleating.

But when she awoke,
she found it a joke,
for they were still a-fleeting.

Then up she took her little crook,
determined for to find them.
She found them indeed,
but it made her heart bleed,
for they'd left all their tails
behind them.

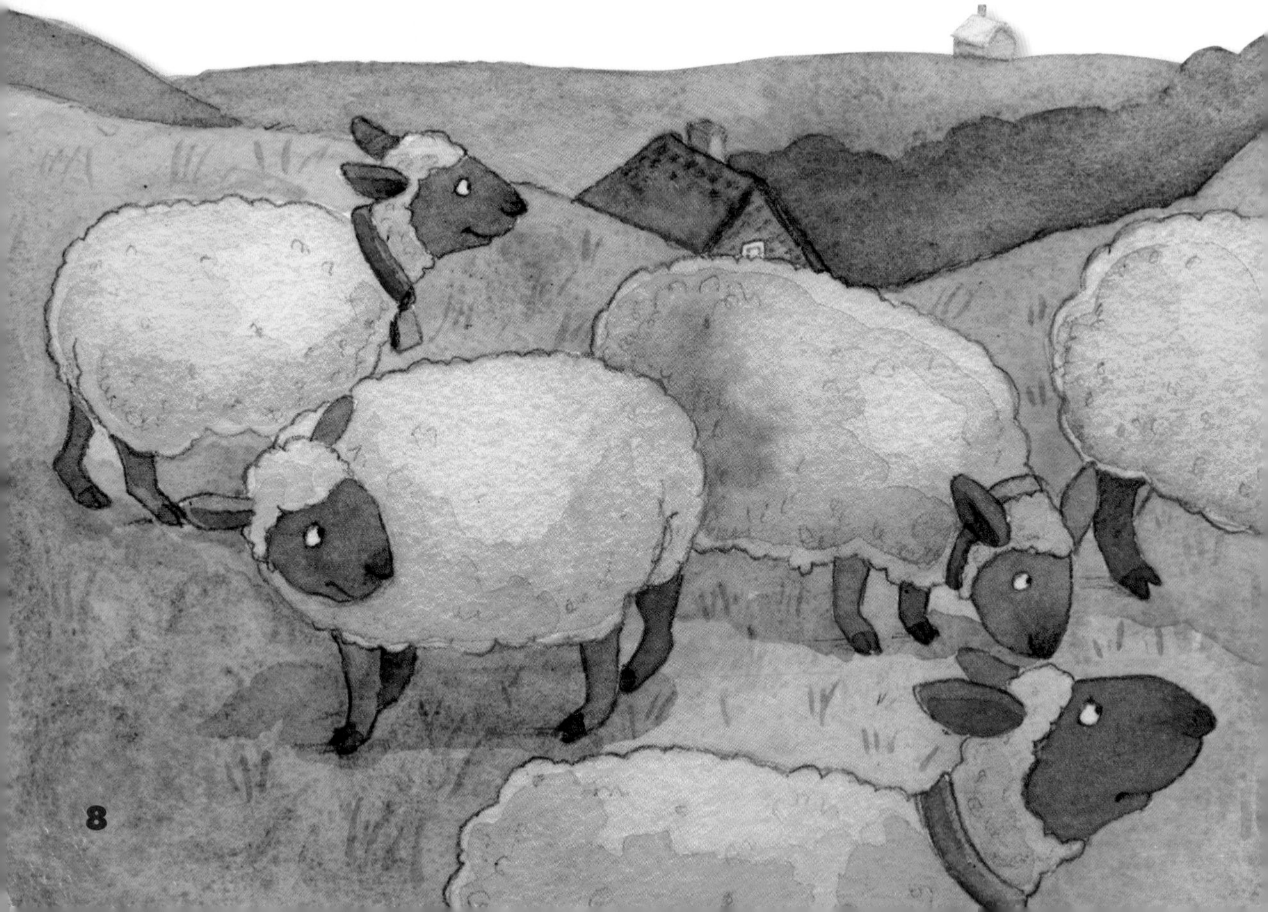

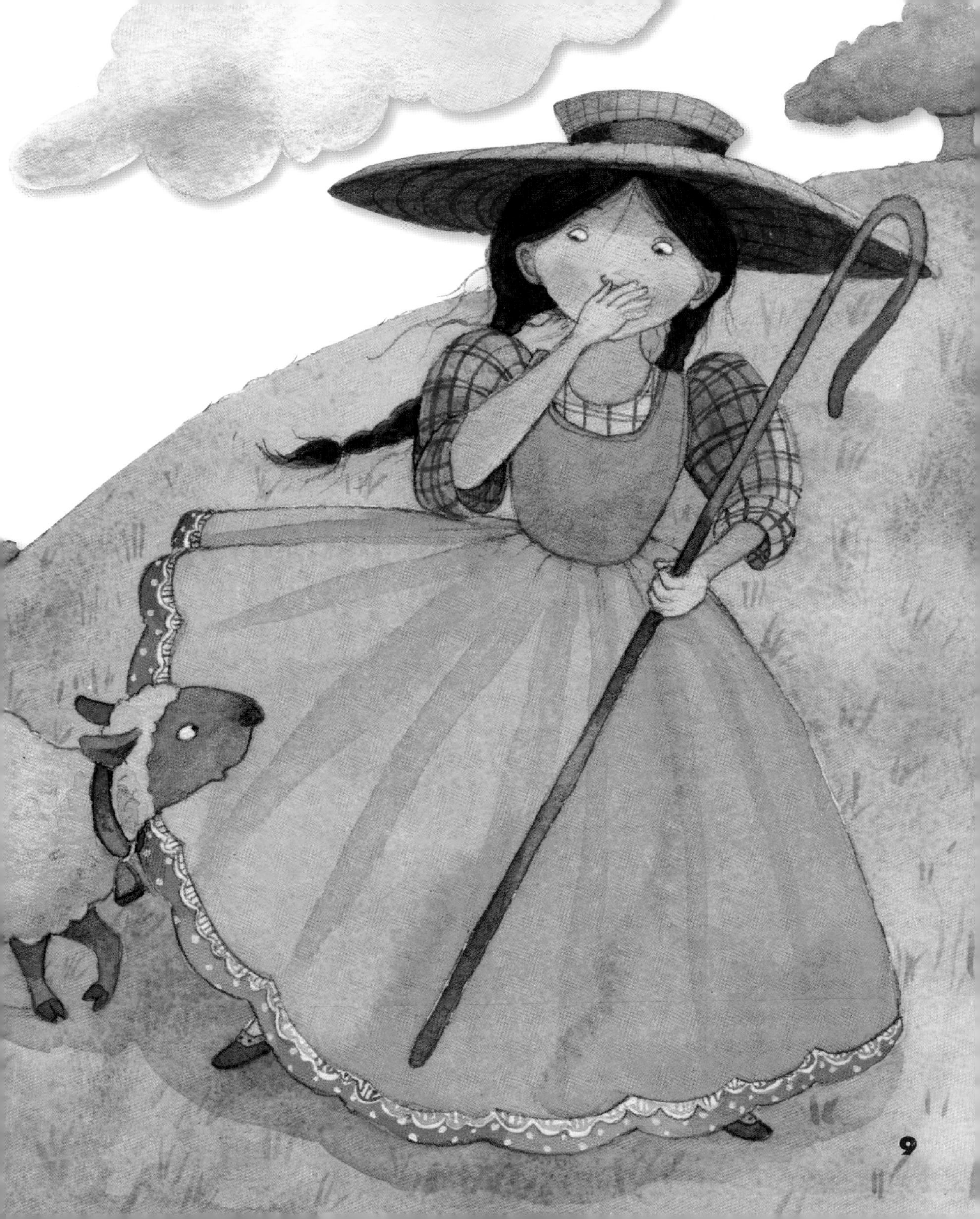

It happened one day,
as Bo Peep did stray
into a meadow hard by.

There she espied
their tails side by side,
all hung on a tree to dry.

She heaved a sigh
and wiped her eye,
and over the hillocks
went rambling.

And tried what she could,
as a shepherdess should,
to tack each again
to its lambkin.

ABOUT MOTHER GOOSE

We all remember the Mother Goose nursery rhymes we learned as children. But who was Mother Goose, anyway? Did she even exist? The answer is . . . we don't know! Many different tales surround this famous name.

Some people think she might be based on Goose-footed Bertha, a kindly old woman in French legend who told stories to children. The inspiration for this legend might have been Queen Bertha of France, who died in 783 and whose son Charlemagne ruled much of Europe. Queen Bertha was called Big-footed Bertha or Queen Goosefoot because one foot was larger than the other.

The name "Mother Goose" first appeared in Charles Perrault's *Les Contes de ma Mère l'Oye* ("Tales of My Mother Goose"), published in France in 1697. This was a collection of fairy tales including "Cinderella" and "Sleeping Beauty"—but these were stories, not poems. The first published Mother Goose nursery rhymes appeared in England in 1781, as *Mother Goose's Melody; or Sonnets for the Cradle*. But some of the verses themselves are hundreds of years old, passed along by word of mouth.

Although we don't really know the origins of Mother Goose or her nursery rhymes, we *do* know that these timeless verses are beloved by children everywhere!

Liza Woodruff has been illustrating children's books for thirteen years. She lives in Vermont in an old farmhouse with her husband, two children, a cat, a dog, two guinea pigs, and three chickens. Liza is constantly inspired by her children and pets, and the farm country where they all live.